The Boxcar Children® Mysteries

The Boxcar Children
Surprise Island
The Yellow House Mystery
Mystery Ranch
Mike's Mystery
Blue Bay Mystery
The Woodshed Mystery
The Lighthouse Mystery
Mountain Top Mystery
Schoolhouse Mystery
Caboose Mystery
Houseboat Mystery
Snowbound Mystery
Tree House Mystery
Bicycle Mystery
Mystery in the Sand
Mystery Behind the Wall
Bus Station Mystery
Benny Uncovers a Mystery
The Haunted Cabin Mystery
The Deserted Library Mystery
The Animal Shelter Mystery
The Old Motel Mystery
The Mystery of the Hidden Painting
The Amusement Park Mystery
The Mystery of the Mixed-Up Zoo
The Camp Out Mystery
The Mystery Girl
The Mystery Cruise
The Disappearing Friend Mystery

The Mystery of the Singing Ghost
The Mystery in the Snow
The Pizza Mystery
The Mystery Horse
The Mystery at the Dog Show
The Castle Mystery
The Mystery on the Ice
The Mystery of the Lost Village
The Mystery of the Purple Pool
The Ghost Ship Mystery
The Mystery in Washington DC
The Canoe Trip Mystery
The Mystery of the Hidden Beach
The Mystery of the Missing Cat
The Mystery at Snowflake Inn
The Mystery on Stage
The Dinosaur Mystery
The Mystery of the Stolen Music
The Mystery at the Ballpark
The Chocolate Sundae Mystery
The Mystery of the Hot Air Balloon
The Mystery Bookstore
The Pilgrim Village Mystery
The Mystery of the Stolen Boxcar
Mystery in the Cave
The Mystery on the Train
The Mystery at the Fair
The Mystery of the Lost Mine
The Guide Dog Mystery
The Hurricane Mystery

The Pet Shop Mystery
The Mystery of the Secret Message
The Firehouse Mystery
The Mystery in San Francisco
The Niagara Falls Mystery
The Mystery at the Alamo
The Outer Space Mystery
The Soccer Mystery
The Mystery in the Old Attic
The Growling Bear Mystery
The Mystery of the Lake Monster
The Mystery at Peacock Hall
The Windy City Mystery
The Black Pearl Mystery
The Cereal Box Mystery
The Panther Mystery
The Mystery of the Queen's Jewels
The Mystery of the Stolen Sword
The Basketball Mystery
The Movie Star Mystery
The Mystery of the Black Raven
The Mystery of the Pirate's Map
The Ghost Town Mystery
The Mystery in the Mall
The Mystery in New York
The Gymnastics Mystery
The Poison Frog Mystery
The Mystery of the Empty Safe
The Home Run Mystery
The Great Bicycle Race Mystery

The Mystery of the Wild Ponies
The Mystery in the Computer Game
The Honeybee Mystery
The Mystery at the Crooked House
The Hockey Mystery
The Mystery of the Midnight Dog
The Mystery of the Screech Owl
The Summer Camp Mystery
The Copycat Mystery
The Haunted Clock Tower Mystery
The Mystery of the Tiger's Eye
The Disappearing Staircase Mystery
The Mystery on Blizzard Mountain
The Mystery of the Spider's Clue
The Candy Factory Mystery
The Mystery of the Mummy's Curse
The Mystery of the Star Ruby
The Stuffed Bear Mystery
The Mystery of Alligator Swamp
The Mystery at Skeleton Point
The Tattletale Mystery

THE MYSTERY AT SKELETON POINT

created by
GERTRUDE CHANDLER WARNER

Illustrated by Hodges Soileau

ALBERT WHITMAN & Company
Morton Grove, Illinois

Library of Congress Cataloging-in-Publication Data
is available from the Library of Congress.

The Mystery at Skeleton Point
created by Gertrude Chandler Warner;
illustrated by Hodges Soileau.

ISBN 0-8075-5519-3(hardcover)
ISBN 0-8075-5520-7(paperback)

Cover art by David Cunningham.

For more information about Albert Whitman & Company,
visit our web site at www.albertwhitman.com.

Contents

CHAPTER   PAGE

1. Not-So-Funnybones   1
2. The Walking Skeleton   14
3. Skullduggery   26
4. The Aldens Have a Dog Day   36
5. A Forbidden Island   48
6. The Hidden Trail   60
7. The Secret in the Library   71
8. Locked Out!   81
9. Skeleton Keys   96
10. Alive in Dead Man's Cave   108

CHAPTER 1

Not-So-Funnybones

The Alden family loved nothing better than long family car trips. They enjoyed playing games, telling stories and jokes, and having roadside picnics. Even in the car, they kept themselves busy with jobs.

Grandfather Alden's main job was driving, of course, plus laughing at his grandchildren's jokes and listening to their plans.

Since twelve-year-old Jessie was the best map reader, her job was to give Grandfather directions.

Benny liked to help Grandfather with directions, too. Now that he was six, Benny could read. His job was to call out the road signs.

"Shady Lake, six miles!" he announced when they passed a sign on their way to visit Grandfather's cousin Charlotte. "How far is that?"

"Way too far," fourteen-year-old Henry joked. He had squeezed himself between Benny and their ten-year-old sister, Violet so the two younger children could have the window seats. Henry's job was to not get twisted into a pretzel while Benny read road signs and Violet wrote in her diary.

"Don't forget to write a page about the scary house," Benny reminded his sister.

Now that the family was almost there, Jessie folded up the map and put it away. She unfolded a news clipping and a letter Grandfather's cousin had sent the week before. "Cousin Charlotte says to watch for a fork in the road right after the general store. There's a dirt road that goes to Skeleton Point if we want to stop. The other road goes to town."

"Read the spooky part again," Benny begged Jessie. "About the skeleton and the statues with no hands near the house at Skeleton Point."

"I can't, Benny. I have to watch the road," Jessie said. "Besides, the article she sent is mainly about her buying Skeleton Point, and some silly things people said about the skeletons that are in the house."

Grandfather drove slowly, looking for the turnoff. "Back when Charlotte and I were young, a real family lived there, not just skeletons for the medical school," Grandfather said. "The two of us often rowed across the lake to Skeleton Point. We never did get a good look at the property itself, but now that Charlotte owns it, we will!"

"Why is it called Skeleton Point?" Benny asked.

Grandfather smiled in the rearview mirror. "Some local people used to say there was a burial vault on the property. But it turns out the whole family is buried in the town cemetery. I don't think there's any such thing."

"What about the Walking Skeleton?" Benny asked. "Did you ever see that?"

Grandfather chuckled again. "Oh, that tale is something new — probably just someone pulling a prank. Charlotte said the story has to do with Dr. Tibbs's skeleton collection. He was the last owner before Charlotte bought the place. He collected skeletons for the medical school. I gather he sometimes put them in the windows to scare off trespassers."

A few minutes later, Benny forgot all about skeletons when he spotted his favorite kind of road sign: ICE CREAM AHEAD. "Can we stop? Lunch was a long time ago."

Everyone in the car laughed. For Benny, lunch always seemed like a long time ago.

Grandfather pulled up in front of the Shady Lake General Store. The Aldens got out to stretch their legs.

Violet sniffed the fresh air. "I like that woodsy pine smell. Now I know we're really on vacation."

"I like stopping for ice cream," Benny

said. "That's how *I* know we're really on vacation."

The children entered the old store. They made their way past fishing poles, garden rakes, and camping goods. When they came to a freezer full of homemade ice cream, they lined up behind the other customers who were also waiting for cones.

Nearby, several older men and women sat in a booth. They were playing cards and eating ice cream with long spoons.

While he waited, Benny tried not to stare.

"Well, young fellow, I hope you're not trying to see what cards I'm holding," one of the cardplayers said with a twinkle in his eye. "Your eyes are bigger than my ice-cream bowl."

Benny felt his ears get red. "Are you playing Go Fish?" he asked. "That's what we played in the car when we drove from Greenfield. Only now it's time for Go Eat Ice Cream, not Go Fish."

Everyone at the table chuckled.

"I'm getting chocolate ice cream," Benny continued. "And know what? We're going to Skeleton Point. Grandfather's cousin Charlotte bought it — even the skeletons. She asked us to help her fix up the house. We might even get to stay there overnight."

The players looked up from their cards when they heard this.

"Well," one silver-haired lady said, "you must be very brave. A lot of strange things have been going on at Skeleton Point ever since Charlotte bought Dr. Tibbs's old place."

Another man at the table put his finger to his lips. "Now, don't go scaring the boy with all that foolish talk about the Walking Skeleton."

The woman ignored the man. "Well, don't say we didn't warn you. I heard from William Mason, who's working out there, that there's a skeleton in the house trying to turn into a real person again. If you ask me, that's why some of those statues have missing parts."

Now Benny's eyes were bigger than dinner plates.

"Pay no attention," another cardplayer told Benny. "Everything's been falling down at Skeleton Point for years, especially those statues. I was glad to hear Charlotte's going to fix up the place. That'll stop all this Walking Skeleton nonsense."

"Maybe the Walking Skeleton is a real person already," Benny said. "I'm a walking skeleton, too. Only I have muscles on top of my skeleton."

The cardplayers laughed again and returned to their game.

When the Aldens got their cones, they sat on the front porch of the general store to enjoy their ice cream.

"Where to next?" Grandfather asked when everyone had finished. "As if I didn't know."

"Skeleton Point!" the children cried at the same time.

"Skeleton Point it is," Grandfather said.

Soon he slowed down when he came to a hand-painted sign nailed to a tree. A picture of a skull and words painted in dripping red paint warned, SKELETON POINT — KEEP OUT.

"Does that mean us?" Henry asked.

"Not at all," Grandfather said. "Charlotte said if we want to take a look at her property, we can go anytime. She keeps the driveway closed off to discourage trespassers. I'll park down here while you children run up and take a quick look around."

Violet zipped up her jacket. "See you in a little bit, Grandfather."

"It's so quiet," Benny said in a hushed voice as they walked through the dark, misty woods.

The next moments were not quiet at all, as a burst of barking broke the silence.

Startled, Benny grabbed his sister's arm.

"It's okay," Jessie said. "It's a dog."

A chocolate-brown Labrador retriever, bounded toward the children, gave one last bark, then ran off.

"I'm glad that was just a dog, not the Walking Skeleton!" Benny said as they approached the house.

"Whoa, maybe *that* is!" Henry pointed to a bony figure moving toward the mansion. As they watched, the figure vanished.

The children froze. Jessie and Henry tip-toed toward the house.

"Whoever — or whatever — that was is gone," Jessie said when she came back for Benny and Violet. "There's nobody around. Come see the house. It's a little spooky, but beautiful, too."

Indeed it was. The children passed an empty reflecting pool full of leaves. On each side stood several moss-covered statues — goddesses, cherubs, angels, even a stone lion. The figures were cracked, and a couple of them were missing arms or hands.

"It's so sad that they're all crumbling and ruined," Violet said when she came closer.

Close up, the stone house wasn't as big as it looked from a distance. Its long windows and tall doors made it seem larger than it really was.

"The house will be so pretty after it's fixed up," Violet said as they walked along the stone porch.

Henry saw something dark hanging off the stone railing. He held up a long black T-shirt painted with a skull on the front and skeleton bones on the back. "What's this doing here?"

"What are *you* doing here?" a strange voice said from somewhere nearby.

The children heard thrashing again, then a splash in the distance. But no one appeared, and the voice did not speak again.

Henry hung the T-shirt on the railing. "We'll have to tell Charlotte there's a trespasser on her property. And that one didn't sound like a dog."

Jessie jiggled the doorknobs of several doors, but none of them opened. "I wonder if anyone is inside." She stopped in front of one of the tall windows. When she tried to speak, no words came out.

"What's the matter?" Henry took a few more steps and looked inside. There, peering out of the window, was a skeleton! It stood on bony legs and grinned out at the children. "The Walking Skeleton?" Henry said, in a dry whisper. It took him and Jessie a moment to realize that the old skeleton was harmless. "Hmm. Well, it's certainly not walking anywhere," Henry said, noticing the wire that held it up.

Finally, Jessie found her voice again. "It must be one of those medical skeletons Grandfather told us about," she whispered, so the younger children wouldn't hear. "Let's show it to Benny and Violet right away so they don't get a sudden surprise."

"Good idea," Henry agreed. "Hey, guys, come over here if you want to see what a complete skeleton looks like. It's one of the ones Dr. Tibbs must have used to teach students at the medical school."

Benny and Violet walked over to the window.

"Oooh." They stared at the skeleton staring back at them.

"Oooh," an owl — or something that sounded like an owl — echoed in the distance.

Jessie went down the back steps. "Let's see if this path leads to the lake."

The children walked along until the

path ended on a point overlooking the lake. From there, a set of wooden steps led to a small, sandy beach below. A yellow rowboat bobbed on a dock.

A loud splash broke through the silence.

"Aaah!" the Aldens cried.

Something much larger than any duck — and much hairier — broke the surface of the still, foggy lake.

Benny took Jessie's hand. "What was that?"

The hairy creature disappeared under the water again just as more fog rolled in.

"Maybe the Walking Skeleton turned into a swimming skeleton," Benny said.

Jessie squeezed Benny's hand. "Don't worry, it's just a swimmer." But she wasn't so sure.

The children took one last look at the mist-covered lake, then hurried back to Grandfather and his warm, cozy car.

CHAPTER 2

The Walking Skeleton

"Goodness," Grandfather said when his grandchildren returned from Skeleton Point. "You look as if you've seen a ghost."

"Not a ghost, Grandfather — a monster in Shady Lake!"

"Goodness, that must have been quite a fright," Grandfather said. "What about the Walking Skeleton?"

"We found a skull T-shirt hanging off the porch," Henry answered. "And one of Dr. Tibbs's skeletons was hanging in a window, too."

"You'll have to tell Charlotte all about your sightings." Grandfather turned onto the main road and headed to the town of Shady Lake. "She'll want to hear everything. Here we are."

Grandfather pulled into the driveway of a snug blue house set behind a garden full of flowers. Cousin Charlotte, who was tall and white-haired like Grandfather, stood in the garden talking with an older man.

When she saw the Aldens' car pull in, Charlotte quickly came over to the car.

"Oh, James — and your wonderful grandchildren! I'm so happy you're here at last," Cousin Charlotte cried. "I've been gardening out front so that I would spot you right away. Come meet my visitor." She turned to the man she had been speaking to. "James, this is William Mason. William, this is my cousin, James Alden, and his delightful grandchildren, Henry, Jessie, Violet, and Benny Alden."

Jessie smiled and put out her hand for a handshake. "Oh, someone at the general store mentioned your name," she said.

Mr. Mason didn't smile back, shake hands, or seem the least bit interested in Jessie or any of the Aldens.

"I guess we'll have to finish our business some other time, Charlotte," he finally said before opening the garden gate to leave. "I see you're too busy with all these people to discuss business right now."

Cousin Charlotte didn't let this stop her. "Actually, I'm glad you're here, William. When I heard my cousin was driving up this way on business, I asked him to bring along the children to help at Skeleton Point, too. I'd like nothing better than to have you work with them. There are so many things they can do."

Mr. Mason stared at Charlotte before he finally spoke. "Well, if children are involved, I'm not sure you need a trained architect like me. I'll see you in the morning to discuss these plans. Good day."

Before Charlotte could say another word, Mr. Mason headed down the street.

Grandfather gave Cousin Charlotte a

hug. "I'm sorry if we interrupted something important."

Charlotte gave the children the same welcoming Alden smile Grandfather often gave his grandchildren. "Not to worry, James. William and I were just winding up when you arrived. After he read in the paper that I had bought Skeleton Point, he contacted me to see if I needed help. I'm very lucky to have him, since he's a retired architect. He specialized in old buildings."

Benny could hardly stand still now that he had something exciting to tell Charlotte. "How about old skeletons?" he asked. "He'd better like those when he's at Skeleton Point, 'cause, know what? That's what's out there. We saw a real skeleton staring out the window and a hairy monster in the lake."

Charlotte's soft blue eyes widened in surprise. "Goodness, something in the lake, too? The one you saw in the window is Mister Bones. Sorry if he gave you a scare," Charlotte told the children. "I left him hanging there to keep trespassers away from the house, just like Dr. Tibbs used to do. But I didn't think there was a *monster* in the lake." Cousin Charlotte laughed. "What did it look like?"

Jessie explained about the T-shirt Henry had found on the porch railing and the swimmer with the long hair.

"Don't forget the barking dog," Benny reminded Jessie.

Charlotte chuckled. "Oh, that was probably Greeny Owen's dog, Max. And Greeny himself was the swimmer, most likely. He was once a student of Dr. Tibbs. He never did finish medical school, but he knows more about bones than most doctors. Local people have told me he's quite upset that I bought the property. Over the years, he's come to think of it as his. He works in a lab at the medical school and often swims or rows over from the island, where he lives with Max."

"Does he have lots of hair?" Benny wanted to know.

"Well, Max has short hair, and Greeny has long hair — for a man, that is," Charlotte explained. "Plus a little skull earring. He often wears that black T-shirt with the skull and skeleton on it. He must have taken it off to go swimming. Nobody but Greeny would go swimming on such a damp, chilly day."

"He didn't scare us." Benny felt brave now that he had arrived at Charlotte's cozy house. "Not a bit."

Charlotte hugged Benny, then gave each of the other children a hug, too. "Well, I'm glad of that. I can't seem to make a friend of Greeny yet. I'm hoping you children will have better luck. He knows so much about Dr. Tibbs's skeleton collection. I'd love to ask him to organize it before I send it on to the medical school. Unfortunately, he disappears on me whenever I go over to Skeleton Point."

"That's what he did with us," Henry said. "Disappeared right under the water."

As Charlotte led the children to a greenhouse in back of her house, she told the children more about Greeny. "I suppose I should be glad that he and Max do such a good job of guarding the property. The problem is, he chases off everyone, including the locksmith I sent over last week! Maybe the four of you will have better luck getting to know him and Max."

"We like dogs," Jessie said. "Especially watchdogs. Our dog, Watch, guarded us when we lived in a boxcar we fixed up in the woods after our mother and father died. Now Watch watches out for us at Grandfather's house."

Charlotte put her arm around Jessie. "I'm so glad Watch — and Cousin James — found you. Now, here's another house for you to live in while you're here — my old greenhouse. I didn't need all of it for plants, so I turned the rest of it into a guest cottage. See?"

"Oh." Violet was so pleased when she walked into the all-glass building, she hardly knew what to say. "We'll be able to see the stars and moon at night."

"And the moon and stars will be able to see you — at least when this foggy weather blows away." Charlotte led the children to the far end of the greenhouse. "You can put your sleeping bags down on these camp cots. You're also welcome to sleep out at Skeleton Point anytime. There are several decent beds in the tower of the house. Just bring your sleeping bags."

"Too bad the rest of us have to sleep in a house with a roof you can't see through," Grandfather joked. "You've done a wonderful job with this greenhouse, Charlotte. We certainly spent a lot of happy hours in here when we were children. Now it's my grandchildren's turn to have some fun in here."

"I hope so," Charlotte said. "Now come inside my real house for some cookies and lemonade. You children must be starving."

"I sure am," Benny said as if he had completely forgotten the ice-cream cone he'd polished off just a little while before.

The children followed Charlotte through the back garden and into her kitchen. Just as everyone sat down, the phone rang.

"Help yourselves," Charlotte said before she went to answer it.

The children passed around a basket of

oatmeal cookies. While they munched, they could hear Charlotte speaking with someone about Skeleton Point and the Aldens.

"You'll love Cousin James's grandchildren," they heard Charlotte say. "They are very grown-up and love hard work. They once fixed up an old boxcar in the woods and lived in it."

Charlotte looked a bit more thoughtful when she returned. "Sorry I took so long. That was Hilda Stone. She's an artist who just opened a studio in Shady Lake. William hired her to assist with the artworks that came with the Skeleton Point property," Charlotte said. "I must say, the two of them have some very definite opinions about the work out there and how it should be done. Sometimes they forget that I'm the owner!"

"Violet's an artist, too," Henry said. "If you need any drawings or pictures, Violet's the one to ask."

Charlotte nodded. "That's just what your grandfather told me on the phone. I'd love to have you children photograph and draw some of the artworks at Skeleton Point so

I can have some before-and-after pictures. The statues are just crumbling to pieces, especially lately. That's how all the Walking Skeleton stories got started."

Benny put down his cookie. "A lady at the general store said the Walking Skeleton takes arms and hands from the statues so it can turn into a person again!"

"That's one of the tales going around, but, of course, it's just a story," Charlotte said. "I really don't know how the statues got damaged recently. They are quite old and already worn away by the weather. But now a few pieces are missing — not just falling off, but disappearing. I do hope you can all keep an eye on the property."

This gave Jessie a good idea. "We gave Benny an instant camera for his birthday. If we take pictures of the statues and something happens to them, maybe we can figure out when it happened and who was around at that time."

"Excellent," Charlotte said. "I'll be dropping off a job list tomorrow morning with Hilda and William. I'll make sure to tell them to let you children photograph and sketch around the property. That will give them more time to do other things."

"Here's to catching the Walking Skeleton!" Jessie said.

The Aldens clinked their lemonade glasses.

CHAPTER 3

Skullduggery

By the time the Alden children tucked themselves into bed in the greenhouse, a steady breeze was blowing in from Shady Lake. The children gazed up through the glass ceiling and walls. Branches on Charlotte's willow tree gently swayed back and forth, back and forth. Soon all four children were sound asleep.

But they did not sleep through the night. At four in the morning, a crack of thunder shook the greenhouse. Seconds later, streaks of lightning lit it up.

Jessie sat up first, after she heard some barking. "Watch!" she said, when she thought she saw a dog outside the greenhouse. She rubbed her eyes. "Oh, we're at Charlotte's, not at home."

Soon loud plops of rain pelted the greenhouse.

Henry pulled his pillow around his ears. "What a racket!"

Benny scrunched himself way down into his sleeping bag. "Make the noise go away."

Violet leaned over from her cot and patted Benny. "They're only raindrops. Oh, no, what's that?" Violet asked when she saw something move outside the greenhouse.

By the time Jessie looked out, the lightning was over and everything was completely dark again. "I think the lightning played tricks on our eyes. We'd better go back to sleep."

The noisy raindrops gave way to a gentle rain, and everyone fell asleep again. An hour and a half later, the greenhouse filled with light.

"It's only five-thirty," Henry said when he

checked his watch. "It's so bright in here."

Jessie yawned and stretched. "I dreamed Violet saw somebody with a dog outside during the storm. I thought Watch had followed us to Shady Lake."

The Aldens quickly dressed and rolled up their sleeping bags. They had a big day ahead.

Charlotte was enjoying a cup of coffee with Grandfather when the children entered the kitchen. "Good morning," Charlotte said, passing around a basket of blueberry muffins. "Take as many as you like," she told the children. "Cousin James said you brought your bikes with you and want to bike out to Skeleton Point today instead of having us drive you there. It's several miles each way on the bike path. You're welcome to take out my rowboat, too. It's the yellow one tied to the dock below Skeleton Point. You're going to need a lot of energy for all your activities, so eat up."

"We will," Henry said as he buttered his muffin. "Are you and Grandfather going to come with us?"

"Not today, children," Grandfather answered. "Charlotte and I have another cousin who lives upstate. She's been feeling poorly, so we're leaving for a few days, after Charlotte stops off at Skeleton Point."

Charlotte put down her cup. "I'm going to meet with William and Hilda on the way. I'll tell them I want you children to photograph and sketch the gardens and the house inside and out."

After the children made their lunches, they went to get their bikes in Charlotte's toolshed. That's when they got an awful shock.

"What's this?" Henry asked when he pulled his helmet from his bike bag. "Did you guys play a trick on me?" Inside Henry's helmet, a plastic Halloween skull grinned back at him.

"Hey! There's a skull in my bike helmet, too! And in yours and yours," Benny said, pointing to the grinning plastic skulls inside his sisters' helmets. "Somebody played a joke, but it wasn't me."

When Charlotte came out, she didn't find

the joke quite as funny, though she tried to laugh about it. "Goodness. I guess I can always use them at Halloween for my trick-or-treaters."

Benny turned one of the skulls upside down to see if anything was inside. "We got the trick but not the treat."

Charlotte laughed. "Well, if you children need more treats than what I left out for your lunches, stop at the general store. The bike path runs right behind it. You'll see a sign for it."

"Goody," Benny said. "I saw lots of snacks there yesterday."

The children put on their helmets and set off for the bike path. Since it was still early, they had it to themselves for a while.

Jessie checked the small bike mirror on her handlebars and saw a jogger in the distance. "I guess runners use this path, too," she told the others. "There's somebody behind us."

When Henry turned around to take a look, the jogger took off into the woods. "Whoever it was is gone."

The children rolled along, making good time on the smooth, empty path.

"There's the sign for the general store. Should we stop?" Jessie teased, even though she already knew the answer.

"I saw gorp fixings in the store — nuts, raisins, and chocolate chips," Henry said.

"Good, gorp," Benny said about the delicious, healthy snack they often brought on their outings.

The general store was already busy with people buying fishing tackle, getting mail, drinking coffee, and picking up groceries and the morning newspaper.

Jessie led the way to the camping section. "Here are the nuts and raisins. Benny, you and Violet go over to the baking aisle for the chips. I brought along some zip bags so we can mix up some gorp for each of us."

When Benny and Violet came to the next aisle, a young woman was blocking the way. She and one of the cardplayers the children had seen the day before were so busy talking, they didn't see the children standing there.

"Have you lived here a very long time?" the young woman asked the man, who was wearing a fishing vest today. "I'm trying to get information about those statues out at Skeleton Point. Nobody seems to know how old they are or where they came from."

"Or where some parts of the statues are going," the man told the young woman. "Lots of fool stories are going around about somebody — or something — damaging the statues. Stay away from them, I say. Those old statues have been out there forever — before I was born, anyway. Leave 'em be. Why do you want to know?"

The young woman hesitated, then stopped to read the label on a jar of honey. "Um . . . just curious."

With that, the young woman left the store without buying anything.

"Newcomers!" the man told Benny and Violet when he saw them standing there. "Always asking questions. You'd think from

that young lady that Shady Lake was nothing but old statues covered with moss.
What about our fishing? Why, our trout are
practically jumping out of the lake."

"They are?" Benny asked, hoping to find
out where he could see some of these jumping trout.

The man left without answering Benny.

"All set?" Jessie said when she and Henry
joined the younger children. "Let's go pay
for everything."

While the children stood in line, they
heard a grinding sound nearby. One of the
clerks was making keys for a customer.
"Here's the extra key you wanted, Greeny."
The worker handed over a new key and a
brown bag. "Bring it back if it doesn't fit
this lock you just bought."

"That must be Greeny Owen!" Henry
whispered to his brother and sisters.

"I guess even on the island you have to
be careful to keep your cabin locked up,
huh?" the clerk asked.

"Um . . . right." Greeny pocketed the key
and put the bag in the small backpack he

wore over his T-shirt and jogging shorts. He stepped away from the counter and left.

"I think Greeny was the jogger I saw in my bike mirror," Jessie said quietly.

Henry agreed. "I bet you're right. I wonder why he ran into the woods when I turned around. It was almost like he was following us but didn't want us to see him."

After the children made up their gorp bags, they returned to the parking lot.

Benny poked Henry, then Jessie. "See that lady getting in the red car? She was being nosy about the statues when she was talking to that fisherman," Benny said.

Henry watched the woman back out her red car and head down the road. "There sure are a lot of people besides Charlotte interested in those statues."

CHAPTER 4

The Aldens Have a Dog Day

After a long bike ride, the Aldens finally came to Skeleton Point. Just as the children slowed down, a familiar dog bounded from the bushes and barked. Then he began to sniff around.

"He smells our ham sandwiches," Benny guessed.

"There, there, Max," Jessie said softly.

The dog tilted his head the way Watch always did when someone knew his name and spoke gently to him.

Jessie carefully reached into her bike bag.

She found her ham sandwich and tossed a piece of it to Max. This calmed him right away. When the dog whined for more, Jessie tossed another piece farther off. The children didn't have to worry about the dog now.

"I'm glad that worked," Jessie said. "I wonder if Greeny knows his dog is loose."

The next thing the children heard was somebody yelling and whistling. "Max! Maxilla! Get over here!"

"What kind of a name is Maxilla?" Benny wanted to know.

Henry laughed. "It's part of a jawbone. I guess it's a good name for a dog whose owner wears a skull shirt."

"Max!" the children heard again. This time the dog dashed off into the woods to join Greeny.

A few minutes later, when the children rounded the point, they saw Max and Greeny about to get into a rowboat. Then Greeny disappeared into some trees and returned with a blue milk crate. That, too, went into the boat. He whistled for Max to jump in. Soon he and Max headed out to an island a short distance from shore.

"I wonder why he docked at Skeleton Point instead of closer to the general store," Henry said. "From the looks of it, that milk crate seemed pretty heavy."

Jessie wondered the same thing. "Do you think it came from Skeleton Point?"

Violet didn't want to believe anything bad about Greeny. "Maybe he had some personal things he had left with Dr. Tibbs and came by to get them back."

"There's only one way to find out," Henry said. "We'll have to keep an eye on Greeny Owen."

A few minutes later, Henry pulled his bike off the path. "We'll never get our bikes up these steps. Let's tie them up to some trees."

After the children locked their bikes, they began their climb up the wooden steps that went to the top of Skeleton Point.

"Hey, look, there's a shortcut off this path," Benny said when the children had gone halfway. "Can we see where it goes?"

"Sure," Henry said. "After you."

When he came to a small clearing at the far end of the overgrown gardens, Benny spotted someone up ahead sitting on a rock. "Who's that?"

The children walked toward the person.

"Maybe it's Hilda Stone," Violet said. "I hope so. I'd like to meet a real artist."

Something seemed odd to Jessie. "It's funny that person doesn't hear us and turn around. Hello!" she called out. "We're here."

"She's as still as a statue," Violet whispered.

Benny ran ahead. "It *is* a statue — of a girl sitting on a rock," he said. "We sure got fooled."

Violet went up to the statue. The small figure seemed to be gazing at the lake. "She looks so sad. I wonder who it's supposed to be. This one isn't broken like the others." Violet walked around the statue, studying it from every side. "There's a name carved on the back: *Clover Dodge.*"

"Can I take a picture of you next to it?" Benny asked Violet.

"Sure." Violet sat next to the statue. "That's what we planned to do anyway. Later I want to sketch this one. It's beautiful."

"Say cheese," Benny said, but Violet just sat peacefully looking out at the lake, not thinking of cheese at all.

A few minutes later, the children huddled around Benny to wait for the instant picture to appear.

"Oh, it's so beautiful," Jessie said to Violet. "I wonder who Clover Dodge was."

The children walked toward the house. Along the way, they posed next to some of the other statues.

"Hey, my camera's stuck!" Benny complained when he aimed it at Henry, who was imitating the stone lion near the house.

Jessie came over to take a look. "That's because you're out of film, silly. Let's go inside. By now Charlotte must have dropped off the job list. I don't see any cars, but maybe William and Hilda parked by the road."

This time, when they passed Mister Bones in the window, the children waved at

him as if they were used to seeing full-sized skeletons every day.

"Hi, Mister Bones," Benny said. "I'll have to take your picture another time."

Inside, the whole house seemed to creak with every step the children took.

Henry led the way. "Ugh. What was that?" he asked when something brushed against his face. "I hope it wasn't a bat."

The children looked up.

"Eew, it's a long, dusty cobweb," Jessie said.

The children crept along, trying not to walk into any more sticky cobwebs. They soon found the room with Mister Bones hanging in the window. Every corner of Dr. Tibbs's study was full of all kinds of skeletons and skulls — little mouse skulls, the skull from a horse, and many bird and animal skeletons of different sizes.

Violet went over to a delicate bird skeleton.

"Don't even think of touching that," a voice said.

The children whirled around. In the

doorway, the sunlight streaming from behind outlined a person's shape. The Aldens
couldn't quite see who it was.

"What are you doing in here?" the person demanded.

Jessie stepped forward. "We're waiting
for someone. This is our grandfather's
Cousin Charlotte's house. She told us to
come here. We're meeting her friends,
Hilda Stone and William Mason."

"I'm Hilda Stone," the person said.

"Great!" Jessie said. "We were looking
for you, and here you are! We didn't see any
cars outside."

As the tall, brown-haired young woman
stepped forward, the children could see she
seemed unhappy when she saw them standing there. "I parked my car on the road and
walked up a little while ago. The driveway
is chained off so trespassers won't drive
onto the property and poke around where
they don't belong."

Henry swallowed hard before he spoke.
"Charlotte gave us permission. I'm Henry
Alden. These are my sisters, Jessie and Vi-

olet, plus my brother, Benny. Charlotte asked us to help out, just like you."

Hilda Stone took a long time before speaking. "Well, William Mason hired me because I'm a trained artist. A historical house, with so many art treasures, requires experts, not children running about."

Benny felt brave even though Hilda Stone was a little bit scarier than Mr. Bones. "We weren't running. We took our bikes, then we walked up the path, nice and quiet. Plus, I took pictures of all the statues with my camera."

Henry nudged Benny so he wouldn't say anything more. "What Benny means is we'd like to give Charlotte pictures of the property so she knows what has to be fixed."

Footsteps on the squeaky floors interrupted Henry. A long shadow fell across the floor. "That's hardly something for children to decide," a deep voice said.

Even Hilda Stone jumped back. "William! Goodness, I didn't know you were in the house."

William Mason stepped into the room.

"Been here for an hour. Charlotte stopped by and left us a list of chores to finish before she gets back in a few days."

"Us?" Hilda asked. "Does that mean just you and me or these kids, too?"

"All of us," Jessie said in her own clear voice. "Remember, she told you on the phone that she was sending us out here to work? She told Mr. Mason the same thing. That's why we're here."

Mr. Mason looked down at the paper in his hand. "Well, I'm here because I'm an architect. Hilda is here because she's an artist. Yes, we can certainly put you to work. Why don't you go outside and wait? Hilda and I will discuss how to proceed."

"She's the same lady who was asking all those questions in the store," Benny told Jessie when they went outside. "Only we didn't know she was Charlotte's friend. How come she's not friendly?"

Henry put his arm around Benny. "Don't worry about Hilda. We'll just have to get to know her, I guess. Maybe she'll be friendlier when she sees how hard we work."

But it looked like Henry might be wrong. When Hilda came out to speak with the children, she wasn't at all friendly. "William and I need you to go over to the hardware store across the lake for some special light switches," Hilda told the Aldens. "We're too busy right now to drive there."

Henry thought about this. "That'll take a pretty long time, since we're on bikes. Wouldn't it be faster to go in the car so we can all get started working around here?"

Hilda shook her head. "As I said, we simply don't have time to run errands today. Charlotte told William that you know how to row a boat. Her rowboat is the yellow one down by the dock. Here's the combination for the lock. There are enough life jackets below the seats. Row straight past the island to the buildings on the other side of the lake. One of them is the hardware store. Ask for the owner, Brad."

"Sure thing," Henry said when Hilda handed him the information on a piece of paper. "How do we pay for the switches?"

"Well . . . tell Brad to put the bill on Charlotte's account."

Henry had one more thing to say. "Charlotte said maybe Violet could sketch some of the statues out there — before-and-after pictures, so people can see how Skeleton Point used to be."

Hilda had other plans. "No need for that. William and I have already taken note of the outdoor sculptures. Professionals examine artwork in certain ways."

Violet, who hadn't said very much, spoke up now. "We'd love to learn to do that — if you could teach us, that is."

For a second, Hilda seemed almost interested in Violet's request. Then she looked back at the house. William was on the porch waving for her to come inside. She turned back to Violet. "No, no, I haven't time to teach you children my methods. There's so much else to be done. Right now we need those light switches. As for the statues, they are quite fragile. We can't have you working around them in any way."

CHAPTER 5

A Forbidden Island

The children rowed along, enjoying the lake, the birds flying overhead, and the nice easy sound of the lake lapping against the boat.

"I have to admit, this is kind of fun," Jessie said as she pulled the oars of Charlotte's yellow rowboat through the clear water. "We haven't been rowing for a long time. Make sure to tell me if I'm rowing in the right direction."

Benny, face-to-face with Jessie, gave her directions. "If you go straight, you'll bump

into that island where Greeny lives. I wish we could go there, but he might get mad at us."

Henry scanned the lake with the binoculars. "You're right about that, Benny. Not to mention he'd probably send Max after us."

"May I have the binoculars, Henry?" Violet asked. "I'd like to see what Greeny's house looks like." She soon spotted a small log cabin nestled between some trees. "The island is pretty," she said, "but lonely-looking, too. I wonder what it's like to live out there with no family."

"We'll be passing close by," Henry said. "Maybe we can get a look."

Benny took a turn with the binoculars, too. "Hey! A seal is swimming to our boat!"

The older children laughed.

"Benny!" Henry said. "Seals don't live in freshwater lakes. They're ocean mammals. Maybe it's one of those jumping trout you wanted to see."

Benny handed Henry the binoculars. "Take a look. Something furry, not fishy, is swimming around."

"You know what, Benny? You're right," Henry said, surprised. "I do see a furry head swimming our way. Jessie, row slightly to your right, toward the island."

A few strokes later, Benny's "seal" was so close to the boat, the Aldens saw right away that it was Max.

"Max!" Violet called out. "Come here, boy. It's your friends, the Aldens. Come on, Maxilla!"

Jessie rowed carefully. "I'll get closer to the island," she told her brothers and sister. "I know Labs are good swimmers, but I don't want Max to swim out too far. He might get tired."

Max looked far from being tired. He kept his head well above the water and paddled at a nice steady pace. Pretty soon he was alongside the Aldens' boat.

Benny reached down to pat Max's wet head. "Good boy."

The children heard a loud whistle in the air.

"Yo! Maxilla, get back here!"

"It's Greeny." Henry made a megaphone

out of his hands so Greeny would hear him. "Is it okay to come to shore?"

Greeny yelled back, "I guess so. Otherwise Max'll never come in. Pull up on the beach in front of the flagpole." He then went over to his own boat and covered it with a sheet of canvas.

"Darn!" Henry said. "Now we won't be able to see what was in that milk crate he picked up at Skeleton Point."

Jessie guided the rowboat toward the small, stony beach. Max swam alongside so closely the Aldens could see his four legs paddling through the water in a real dog-paddle stroke!

When the boat glided to the beach, Greeny grabbed the rope hooked to the bow. "Pull up here."

Once he got ashore, Max yipped and barked the way Watch always did after a good swim. The Aldens stood back. They knew very well that when Max shook out his fur, they were in for a big shower.

"We wanted to come here," Violet said, "but we didn't know if you liked company. I guess Max came out to invite us."

"Max and I don't get much company out this way," Greeny told the Aldens. "I figured you kids would be busy at the house with those other people poking around Skeleton Point. Did those two friends of Charlotte chase you away, too?"

"You mean William and Hilda?" Jessie asked. "Well, we thought you and Max were chasing *us* away by scaring us when we went looking around yesterday. We heard somebody say, 'What are *you* doing here?' "

Greeny looked away from the children. "Well, I thought you were trespassers, so I gave you a little scare. There've been problems out there lately."

"Did we scare you off the bike path this morning?" Violet asked, softly.

Greeny looked away and didn't answer.

The Aldens didn't find him scary now in his bright red T-shirt and jogging shorts. Even his skull earring looked like the ones Jessie wore on Halloween. His long hair was tied in a neat ponytail.

"I wasn't scared of you," Greeny told the

children. "I'm just not feeling too friendly toward a bunch of strangers taking over Doc Tibbs's place."

Jessie took a deep breath before she spoke. "It's Charlotte's place now. She's fixing it up."

Greeny's mouth tightened. "It doesn't need fixing up any more than the woods need fixing up. Doc's skeleton collection is one of the most important ones in the country. He taught hundreds of medical and veterinary students. Now people are just going in there, moving things around, and even taking things from his collection."

"Some were stolen?" Violet asked. "We looked at some of the bird and animal skeletons, but we wouldn't touch anything without permission."

This didn't cheer up Greeny at all. "Nobody around here knows enough about skeletons to give anyone permission to look at the skeletons."

"You know enough," Violet said in her quiet way. "Charlotte hopes you'll help organize Dr. Tibbs's collection before she donates it to the medical school where it belongs. She says you always run away from her."

Greeny stroked Max's head while he thought about this. "That's because she acts like she owns Skeleton Point and everything in it."

"Well, she does," Jessie reminded Greeny. "But she wants the collection to be kept together and go to the right place."

Greeny got worked up all over again when he heard this. "The right place was to me. But Doc up and died before he wrote out his will. He told me he was leaving me his collection so I could decide what to do with it. Then Charlotte went and bought the place."

"I bet you didn't know she's using all her savings to fix up everything — the house, the statues, and the gardens," Jessie said. "Charlotte really cares about Skeleton Point."

"Well, so do I," Greeny said. "I've kept a watch on it better than anybody. If it weren't for Max and me, the place would be in worse shape than it is. All this hullabaloo about Walking Skeletons and such — those are just stories to cover up plain old thievery and vandalism."

"What's vandalism?" Benny wanted to know.

"People harming property," Jessie said. "Like Charlotte's statues. She bought them, so they belong to her now."

Greeny disagreed with Jessie. "Those statues were priceless — they can't just be bought." Greeny was finished with the Aldens. "Now I think you should get going. I can see we're never going to see eye to eye on this, that's for sure."

The children walked back to the shore. Henry and Jessie dragged the boat to the water's edge. The children climbed in.

" 'Bye, Greeny," Benny yelled as Henry dipped the oars in the water. " 'Bye, Max."

When the children looked back at the island, they heard Max bark to say good-bye, but Greeny had disappeared into his cabin.

Henry rowed the next leg of the trip

across Shady Lake. The other shore soon came into view. "I can't decide about Greeny," Henry said. "He doesn't seem to think anybody has a right to be at Skeleton Point but him."

Violet, who was trailing her hand in the water, had a soft spot for Greeny. "He just wants to protect the property, I think. Let's try to make friends with him. I just know if we do, he'll help Charlotte."

"That's a very sensible idea, Violet," Jessie said. "The better we get to know him, the better our chances are of finding out who's harming Charlotte's property."

Henry finally reached the small marina. "There's the hardware store Hilda told us about," he said. "We'd better pick up those light switches and get back. We lost a lot of time stopping off to see Greeny."

When the children entered the hardware store, they found the owner at the cash register.

Henry handed the man the piece of paper Hilda had given him. "I hope you're

Brad. Hilda Stone told us to see you about some special light switches. They're for the lights over at Skeleton Point."

"I am Brad," the man said, "but I have no idea what you're talking about, young fellow. I don't carry these light switches and never did. And who's this Hilda Stone person, anyway? Probably one of these city people buying up property who doesn't know a darn thing about what she's doing. Never heard of her."

The Aldens looked at one another. Hadn't Hilda told them to find Brad and pick up the special switches?

"What about William Mason?" Jessie thought to ask. "Do you know him?"

"Who doesn't know William Mason?" the man asked. "I'm surprised he volunteered to help fix up that old house. Mason's a fellow who's always trying to make a buck or two. In fact, now that I think about it, he did some talking about wanting to buy the house himself, but Charlotte beat him to it. Doesn't stop him from walking around like he owns the place."

"He does?" Benny asked. "I thought Greeny Owen was the only one who acted like that."

"Greeny?" the man said. "There's another one always creeping around these old places on the lake. Don't know which is worse, the newcomers or the old-timers who think everything on the lake should stay the same as it was a hundred years ago. That's Greeny for you. Sorry about the light switches. You need to go to one of the big stores over in North River for those. It was a total waste of time sending you here."

CHAPTER 6

The Hidden Trail

When the children returned to the dock empty-handed, they got a terrible surprise.

"Our boat is floating away!" Jessie pointed to their little yellow rowboat bobbing out on the lake about twenty feet away. "How did that happen? I know I tied it up."

"Wait here," Henry told Violet and Benny. "We're going to swim after it."

In a flash, Henry and Jessie stripped down to their bathing suits and plunged into the water. They were excellent swimmers and reached the boat in no time.

"Whew," Henry said when he caught his breath — and the boat. "That was close. Thank goodness the wind wasn't blowing any harder. The boat didn't get out too far. You climb in, Jessie. I'll swim along while you row back."

"I wonder how the boat got loose," Jessie said when she and Henry reached the dock.

Jessie got out of the boat and walked over to join Violet and Benny, who were talking to a fisherman on the dock. "Somebody let your boat go," said the fisherman. "A fellow was trying to untie his motorboat, but he unlocked yours by mistake. Guess he forgot to lock yours back up again. I tried calling after him, but he just sped right off. Folks can be mighty careless sometimes."

"Which way did he go?" asked Jessie. The fisherman pointed across the lake toward Skeleton Point.

Jessie reached for the binoculars to take a look. She spotted a motorboat heading out. "Look out there." She handed Henry the binoculars. "Doesn't that look like Mr. Mason from behind?"

Henry grabbed the glasses. "I think it is him. I recognize the red hat he had on yesterday. If he had a motorboat, why did Hilda tell us they didn't have time to go to the hardware store?"

Jessie found the towel she'd packed and shared it with Henry. "The sun will have to dry off the rest of us," she said. "If you ask me, those two are trying to keep us away from Cousin Charlotte's property."

"Well, they can't," Henry said. "Hop in, everybody. We're going to follow Mr. Mason back to Skeleton Point."

But Henry couldn't follow the motorboat to Skeleton Point. It sped right past there without stopping.

"He must be docking someplace else," Jessie said. "That gives me an idea. Instead of going back to Skeleton Point, let's row to that cove we passed not too far from the general store. We'll hike up from there. If Hilda and William don't spot our boat coming in, we'll have a chance to see what they're up to before they expect us back."

Henry didn't need to think twice about Jessie's good suggestion. He dipped one oar into the water and headed for the deserted cove.

After they pulled up, the children dragged the boat as far onto shore as they could.

The woods were still as the Aldens crept along. They soon came to a broken fence that surrounded Skeleton Point.

"Let's go in this way," Henry said when he and Jessie found an opening. "I think I see a trail on the other side."

Once the children were on the property again, they followed the overgrown path that curved around the hillside. With Jessie leading the way, the children hiked single file, holding branches back for one another.

Violet bumped into Jessie when she suddenly stopped. "What's the matter, Jessie?" Violet asked. "Are we at the end?"

Jessie pointed to a rock up ahead. "Come see this rock face. Doesn't it look like a skull, especially with the way there's some old paint where the eyes and mouth are?"

Henry examined the rock. He found a rusted metal door blocking a wide crack in the rock. The door didn't budge. "This is getting weirder and weirder. It's some kind of cave that somebody put a door on. By the looks of it, it's been here a long time. Let's see where this trail goes. I have a feeling it joins up with that other shortcut we took off the main path."

When Violet and Benny stopped for a drink from their water bottles, Jessie pulled Henry aside. "I didn't want to scare Violet and Benny, but I saw something moving up ahead. It could have been a deer, I suppose. Whatever it was, it ran off in the direction we're going."

"Uh-oh," Henry said. "Here comes Benny. I wonder if he saw it, too."

"There's a big skull up there — a real one! See?" Benny pointed to a horse skull stuck in the notch of a tree right by the footpath.

"Somebody's playing a trick," Jessie said so the younger children wouldn't get too

scared. "Let's leave it there so no one knows we saw it."

Benny liked this idea. "Nobody can scare us away, right, Jessie?"

"Right."

Benny and Violet finished drinking their water. They stayed close to Henry and Jessie. Soon the trail crossed the main path between the beach and the house.

"Let's pick it up on the other side," Henry suggested. "Hilda and William won't expect us from that direction."

"This leads to the garden where the Clover Dodge statue is," Violet said.

But Violet was mistaken. "The statue is gone!" she said when she came to the rock where it had been anchored. "Should we go tell Hilda and William?"

Jessie and Henry exchanged glances.

"Let's see if they tell us first," Jessie suggested. "Maybe they had a good reason to take it. And if they didn't, I don't want them to know right away that we know it's missing. I'd also like to find out who made these fresh footprints."

The children looked down at the ground where the statue had been.

"Whoever was here had on work boots or hiking boots with thick treads on the soles." Henry checked his watch. "We've been gone a long time. Hilda and William will be looking for us. Let's look for them first."

The children hiked through the surrounding woods so they could watch the house without being seen. No one seemed to be around until they approached the empty reflecting pool.

Jessie put her finger to her lips. "Shhh. Stop here. Don't breathe."

They watched Hilda Stone go from statue to statue with a sketch pad and a measuring tape. At every statue, she stopped, measured parts of the statues, then marked something down. When she was done, she returned to the house.

The children backtracked to the steps. They'd gone partway up when Benny stopped suddenly.

There was a full-sized seated skeleton in

front of them on the steps. "The Walking Skeleton!" Benny said.

Henry chuckled. "No, I guess you'd have to call it the Sitting Skeleton. It's just sitting there as if it stopped to take a rest."

"I'm not afraid of Halloween tricks even when it's not Halloween." Benny scurried past the skeleton.

Henry looked very serious. "Now I know someone is trying to scare us away from Skeleton Point again," he said.

"You're probably right, Henry," said Jessie. "But who could it be?"

"William Mason and Hilda Stone," said Benny, almost immediately. "They're mean to us, and they don't want us around."

"You're right, Benny. Remember that man in town said William Mason wanted to buy Skeleton Point for himself? Maybe he's mad at Charlotte for buying it first."

Jessie looked thoughtful. "What about Greeny?" she asked. "We know he doesn't want us around, either — and we know he's taking things from the house. Maybe he wants to scare us away so we won't figure out what he's up to. We should still keep an eye on him."

Henry agreed. "In fact, we should keep an eye on all of them."

When they returned to the house, the Aldens found that William had joined Hilda outside.

Jessie waved. "Hi!" she called out, as if she had come straight from her errand across the lake. "Sorry we took so long. The hardware store was out of those light switches."

Hilda and William kept working. It seemed neither of them wanted to say anything.

Finally Hilda spoke up. "Oh, it turns out we don't need them after all."

William pushed back the brim of his red hat and checked his watch. "Half the day's gone. I don't see much use for you kids sticking around here. Hilda and I are doing some technical work Charlotte asked us to do — not something suitable for children."

"We know how to measure, too" Benny said. "I learned in kindergarten."

Hilda hesitated. "What we're doing is a little more complicated than what you do in school. Now, why don't you children go for a bike ride. Or a swim," she suggested before going into the house.

Henry turned to William. "We already went for a swim," he said. "An unplanned one."

William didn't say anything about untying the Aldens' boat, but he looked away and cleared his throat. "Well, then, go for a planned one this afternoon. Take tomorrow off, too. Everything's under control here."

Before William turned to go into the house, the Aldens looked down. Just as they suspected, William was wearing heavy work boots that left deep prints just like the ones near the statue.

CHAPTER 7

The Secret in the Library

After breakfast the next morning, the Aldens made their lunches in Cousin Charlotte's kitchen. While they were bagging their lunches, the phone rang.

Jessie ran for it, and the other children listened in. "Cousin Charlotte! We're fine. We just got our lunches and extra food ready before we leave for town. Then we're riding to Skeleton Point. We're even going to spend the night since you said it was okay." Jessie handed the phone to Henry.

"No, William and Hilda haven't told us

71

what we'll be doing next," Henry said. "All we did yesterday was run an errand, then we biked home.

Charlotte told them all about her trip with Grandfather. Then she added something surprising. "Before we left yesterday, we came across a plastic skeleton — right by the car!"

"You came across a skeleton yesterday, too? So did we!" Henry said.

After that, the younger children took turns speaking with Cousin Charlotte and Grandfather about some of their adventures the day before. By the time they hung up, they were nearly out of breath.

Henry handed the other children their lunches. "Cousin Charlotte's going to tell William to let us into Dr. Tibbs's study this afternoon. She wants us to count everything so she knows exactly what's there before she sends it to the medical school."

"What about the missing statue?" Violet asked. "Did you mention it to her?"

Henry's face grew serious. "I didn't have the heart to tell her about that yet. I was thinking we could bike to town and visit Hilda's studio. Without William around, maybe she'll tell us what she knows about the statues. So what do you say, guys? Everybody ready?"

Ten minutes later, the children headed into town, biking carefully now that their bikes were loaded down with their sleeping bags and overnight things. They parked their bikes in front of the drugstore to pick up film for Benny.

Benny unzipped his bike bag to get his camera. "Hey, my pictures aren't in here with my camera. They were in my bike bag yesterday."

"Are you sure?" Jessie asked Benny. "Did you leave it unzipped? I hope the pictures didn't fall out while we were biking."

Benny shook his head. "No way. I zipped everything up. Remember? I left the bike bag on the porch when we went out in the boat and picked it up when we got back."

Jessie had a suggestion. "Then the pictures must be out at Skeleton Point. We'll look around when we go there this afternoon."

While Jessie ran into the drugstore to get the film, Henry took out the map Charlotte had given him. "Hilda's studio is the next block over," he said when Jessie came out again. "Let's go see if she's there."

When the children rang Hilda's bell, no one answered. A sign with an arrow pointing to the back of the house read, STUDIO. The children walked along quietly, looking in the windows of the house to see if anyone was around. A sign on the garage door read, STUDIO CLOSED.

Jessie cupped her hands over the tall windows of the studio. Then she waved for the other children to come over and look inside, too.

"The Clover Dodge statue!" Violet whispered when she peeked in.

Hilda was seated at a cluttered worktable facing away from the Aldens. The statue stood in the middle of the table. Also on the table were a life-sized skull and a skeleton of a hand. Hilda was bent over a large drawing pad, sketching a large stone arm that looked familiar to the Aldens.

The children tiptoed away.

"We have to decide what to do next," Jessie said.

"A book I noticed on a shelf in the studio gave me an idea," Violet said. "The title was, *Sculptures of Clover Dodge*. It must be the name of the sculptor who made the statue. My idea is to go to the library and see if we can find out more about Clover Dodge."

"Good thinking," Henry said. "One other thing. I didn't get a real good look, but the stone arm Hilda had in there looked like the missing one from the angel statue."

Jessie checked her watch. "I know. Well, let's get to the library like Violet suggested. It's just down the street."

"Can Henry and I wait for you outside?" Benny asked when the children came to the town library.

"Sure," Violet said, setting off with Jessie. "We'll be back in a while."

When the girls found the librarian, they

handed him the piece of paper with the title of the art book they wanted. "My sister and I are interested in this book about a sculptor named Clover Dodge. The book isn't on the shelf. Do you know when it's due back?"

"Clover Dodge?" the librarian asked. "Isn't it funny how some books aren't checked out for ages, then suddenly everybody wants them at the same time? Clover Dodge was a well-known sculptor at the turn of the last century. But her work disappeared, and people forgot about her." The man checked the library computer. "I see one of our local artists, Hilda Stone, checked it out. It's reserved for William Mason next, but I can reserve it for you after he brings it back."

"Hmm, no," Jessie said. "Thank you anyway."

Minutes later, the girls met their brothers outside and told them what they had discovered.

"Wow! So William is interested in Clover Dodge, too," Jessie said. "I wonder if he and Hilda are up to something together with the statues."

"Let's go back to the studio and find out what Hilda has to say," said Jessie.

The rest of the Aldens nodded in agreement. They were always ready for an investigation.

Henry led the way. "While we're walking, Benny can tell you what we discovered while you and Violet were in the library."

Benny couldn't keep his secret another minute. "The scary rock with the door is called Dead Man's Cave, only there aren't any dead people in it," he announced.

Jessie's and Violet's eyebrows shot up.

Henry grinned at the two girls. "Benny and I went to check old maps in the town hall. There are a couple small caves, not very deep ones, on Skeleton Point. One of them is called Dead Man's Cave. The man we met at the general store works in the land records department. He said that a long time ago kids used to hike up there. He'd heard they'd turned the cave into a hideout or a clubhouse. They called it Dead Man's Cave to scare other kids away."

"But we're not scared," Benny said. "We can go there this afternoon, right, Henry?"

"You bet," Henry said. "But first let's see what Hilda is doing with all those skeletons and statue parts from Skeleton Point."

When the children returned to the studio, the STUDIO CLOSED sign was still on the door. This didn't stop the Aldens.

"Hi, Hilda! It's the Aldens," Jessie yelled as she rapped on the window.

Hilda whirled around, startled to see four pairs of eyes staring at her. She opened the door slightly. "What are you doing here? My studio is closed right now."

Violet looked past Hilda. "Oh, so you have the Clover Dodge statue," she said before the young woman could block her view. "Are you fixing it? I'd love to see how."

Hilda stared at Violet. "I'm not here to teach art classes, Violet. I'm here to . . . well, I haven't time to explain."

Henry, who was taller than Hilda, peered right over her shoulder. "Are you fixing the arm from the angel statue, too? Charlotte will be glad you got started on that."

Hilda studied the Aldens' faces. "What do you mean? William was the one who got me working on the angel statue, not Charlotte. He told me she left most of the decisions up to him." Hilda pushed the door to keep the children back. "I really must get back to my work. I'll see you at Skeleton Point later this afternoon."

The Aldens had a lot more to say, but they never got the chance. After she slammed the door, Hilda walked over to the windows and pulled the shades down one by one.

CHAPTER 8

Locked Out!

As soon as the children got on the bike path again, they tried to figure out their conversation with Hilda.

"We didn't get any answers about the Clover Dodge statue," Violet said.

Henry disagreed. "Oh, but we did. Now we know Hilda definitely took things from Skeleton Point and that she doesn't want us to see them. That's got to be the reason she didn't let us in her studio."

"I guess you're right, Henry," Violet said. "I sure wish the statue was back where it belongs. Since it wasn't broken, why did Hilda bring it to her studio?"

The children pedaled along the lake and thought about what to do next.

"Let's have lunch!" Benny suggested. "That helps me figure out things."

"Lunch always solves everything for you, Benny," Jessie said with a laugh. All the same, she slowed down when she came to the sign for the Shady Lake General Store. "You know, if we stop here, we can — "

"Have an ice-cream cone for dessert!" Benny said.

Jessie smiled. "Exactly!"

The children rolled their bikes to a picnic grove close to the dock that belonged to the general store. As soon as the Aldens took out their sandwiches, a flock of ducks decided to join the children for lunch, too. Not a crumb was wasted as the birds waddled under the picnic table. The children hadn't been seated long when another visitor showed up.

"Max!" Jessie said when Greeny's dog raced over to chase the ducks away. "You smelled our ham sandwiches, didn't you? Where's Greeny?"

Benny slid over to pet Max. "Sorry, the ducks ate the rest of my sandwich. Hey, you're as wet as a duck, too. Were you playing in the water?"

"Greeny's boat is docked out there," Henry said, looking at the marina. "He must be at the store getting supplies. Jessie, are you thinking what I'm thinking?"

Jessie nodded. "There's nothing wrong with just going for a walk on the dock, is there? And if we happen to pass Greeny's boat, we might be able to see if he still has that mysterious crate we saw him carry down from Skeleton Point."

The Aldens didn't waste any time. They gathered up their trash and threw it into a nearby basket. Max followed along, hoping to catch a few forgotten crumbs the ducks might have missed.

Benny dug into his backpack for a ball he often carried. He aimed it toward the dock. "Go get it, Max! Let's follow him. Now we have a good excuse to go near the boat."

"Exactly what I was thinking, Detective Alden," Henry told Benny.

As soon as Max found the ball, he trotted out to Greeny's boat.

Jessie had to laugh. "Max is just like Watch. He likes to bring the ball to a special spot then makes us chase him there."

The children ran after Max.

When he got to the dock, Henry stared into the boat. "Greeny sure keeps a lot of stuff in there. Fishing tackle, life jackets, boxes, a couple of toolboxes, fuel cans, and — "

"A skull!" Benny said in a loud whisper. "See? It's in the milk crate, but it's partway covered up."

The children craned their necks, trying to get a better look under the canvas.

Just as a gust of wind began to lift the covering, Greeny appeared. "What are you kids doing?"

Thank goodness for Max. At that moment, he picked up the ball in his mouth and brought it over to Greeny.

"He wants you to take Benny's ball and

throw it," Jessie said. "We were trying to get it back when Max jumped into your boat with it."

Max suddenly dropped the ball, so Benny reached in and picked it up. Max leaped from the boat, and Benny followed him.

By this time, Greeny got in the boat himself. He quickly tucked the canvas cover tightly over the milk carton. "Max, get back here!" Greeny yelled. "Don't throw that ball near the boat, Benny. Got it?"

"Got it," Benny said, walking toward his bike. He felt so upset at being scolded, he forgot all about his ice cream and finishing the game of fetch with Max.

The children quietly pedaled away, not as happily as before. Awhile later, they came to Skeleton Point.

"Let's push our bikes behind those bushes so everything will be safe," Henry suggested. "We can come back for them later."

"What I want to find out," Jessie said as the children began to climb the steps, "is whether William will let us work in Dr. Tibbs's study."

Halfway up, the Aldens searched for the trail they had hiked the day before.

"Hey, where's the secret path?" Benny asked. "Wasn't it right around here?" He skipped a couple steps ahead then came back down. "The skeleton isn't sitting here, either, like yesterday."

"It's almost as if we dreamed up the secret path," Violet said. "Wait! I know why." She pulled away a tangle of prickly holly branches. "These branches covered it up."

Henry still had on his bike gloves. He tossed the thorny branches aside. "Since no one knows we're here yet, let's check Dead Man's Cave before we go to the house."

The Aldens set out on the secret path. Along the way, they looked for the horse skull they had seen the day before. That, too, was gone. They finally located the hideout door.

"Benny, hand me my flashlight," Henry said, peeking into a crack between the door and the rock. "Even if we can't get inside, the door doesn't quite fit over the cave opening. Maybe I can get a look with my flashlight."

Benny rummaged through Henry's bike bag. "Here."

Henry held his flashlight up to the crack. "Gee, it's not much of a hideout," he said. "Our boxcar was way bigger than this. Hey, wait! Jessie, here, take a look."

Jessie took the flashlight. "Wow! That looks like Mister Bones in there. And the horse skull, too. Plus some statues I never saw before. Come here."

Benny could hardly wait. Since he was shorter than the other children, he saw something they had missed. He waved the flashlight over the floor of the hideout. "Look. Footprints."

"They're still muddy," Violet said when she took a look. "Whoever made them was just here."

The children tried hard to pull open the rusty door but had no luck.

"Let's go up to the house," Jessie suggested. "We can at least see if William made those prints. They sure look like his."

"And these!" Henry pointed to a muddy part of the path. "These footprints look pretty new, too. Let's follow them."

When the children returned to the main path, they followed the muddy footprints up the steps.

Henry covered up the secret path with the holly branches again. "I don't want anybody else to find this trail or even know we found it."

When they reached the top, the children saw William heading to the gardening shed with some clippers in his hand.

Jessie caught up to him. "Hi, Mr. Mason," she said. "Oh, your gardening clippers are just like Grandfather's. So are those leather gardening gloves. Were you out pruning brushes?"

William stared at the clippers in his gloved hand as if he didn't know what they were. He ignored Jessie's question. "I thought you kids said you were going swimming today."

"You said that, not us," Henry replied.

"We came here to help Charlotte. Did she call you about working on Dr. Tibbs's skeleton collection? She wants us to count what's in there."

"Waste of time, if you ask me," William said. "Just ship the whole shebang to the medical school and let them do the job."

Violet had something important to tell Mr. Mason. "Charlotte is putting Greeny Owen in charge of the skeletons before she sends them to the medical school."

"Greeny Owen?" William Mason said. "I chased him off here just this morning when I found him wandering around in the house as if he owned it."

Violet had to defend Greeny. "He just wants to protect Dr. Tibbs's skeleton collection. He thinks someone may have taken some of them recently."

William looked at Violet for a long time. "What do you mean, someone took the skeletons? There's such a jumble of bones in there, who would even know if any of them were missing?"

"Greeny would!" Benny blurted out. "And we saw skeletons in the woods, and so did Grandfather and Charlotte."

William laughed. "Well, everybody knows about the Walking Skeleton," he told the Aldens. "Maybe you should tell Charlotte to stay put in her nice little cottage where she won't be scared by skeletons roaming the woods."

"Charlotte isn't scared of skeletons, walking or not," Jessie said. "She's going to fix up Skeleton Point no matter what."

William walked up the broken steps of the reflecting pool. "Well, you can't say she wasn't warned ahead of time."

Jessie checked her watch. "We'd like to go into Dr. Tibbs's study and do what Charlotte asked us to do."

William didn't look too pleased about this, but he nodded anyway. "Suit yourself. If that's what Charlotte wants, feel free."

But the door to Dr. Tibbs's study wasn't open.

Henry pushed the door with his shoulder. "Maybe it's stuck the way it was the other day." When the door didn't budge, he pushed it with his whole body. Still it didn't open. "Know what? There's a lock on it — a new one," he said. "That's why I can't get it open."

Hilda arrived just as the Aldens were heading out to find William.

Jessie went up to her. "Hi, again. Would you happen to have the key to the study? It's locked. Charlotte wants us to get started organizing the skeleton collection."

Hilda looked puzzled. "Locked? Why would anybody lock up those dusty old things? None of the locks inside the house work anyway. Just push the door hard."

"We already did," Henry said. "This lock is new. Did the locksmith finally come? Charlotte sent one out last week, but he got scared off."

Hilda seemed in a hurry and not in any kind of mood to talk with the Aldens. "Well, since you can't get in there, you won't be able to do whatever job Charlotte suggested. Perhaps you should head home until you hear from her again."

The children looked at one another. Why was this woman always trying to make them go away?

Jessie surprised her brothers and sister by agreeing. "Sure. I guess we will go. See you tomorrow."

When the children got outside, Benny was confused. "Why are we going home? Can't we ask her about my photos?"

Jessie put her arm on Benny's shoulder. "We're only going to pretend to leave. We'll sneak to the other side of the house and see what the two of them are up to."

When the children came outside, they waved at William.

"See you tomorrow," Henry called out loudly. Then in a whisper he said, "And probably a whole lot sooner."

Soon the children were hiking through the woods again. As they circled back, they came up with a plan.

"We have to somehow get upstairs without anyone seeing us," Henry said. "That way we'll get a better view around the property. And in old houses, the sound sometimes travels through the heating vents. We might be able to hear what Hilda and William are up to. They seem to spend all their time either outside or downstairs."

The children hid behind some trees not far from the back of the house. A large clearing stood between the house and the woods. Somehow they were going to have to race through the clearing without being seen.

Jessie took the binoculars to check around the property. "Hilda's out talking with William near the reflecting pool. Okay, now. One by one, we have to scoot into the open and go through the back door. Who wants to go first?"

Benny volunteered. "Say when," he whispered to Jessie.

"Now!" Jessie said. "They're facing away from the house. You go, too, Violet. See that room in the tower? We'll meet you up there. If you hear anyone coming, hide behind the furniture. If you get caught, just say you came back to look for Benny's camera." With that, Jessie gave both of the

younger children a little push. They were across the lawn in a flash.

"Uh-oh, duck," Henry told Jessie. "William just turned around. Gee, he's walking this way. I hope he didn't see us."

But William seemed too lost in his own thoughts to notice Jessie and Henry crouching in the bushes. He passed just a couple feet away from them on his way to the gardening shed.

"It's now or never," Jessie whispered to Henry. "Hilda is putting her sketch pad and pencils back into her tote bag. She's going to turn around any minute."

Henry glanced up at the main house. "Look, Benny and Violet are waving us that the coast is clear." Henry grabbed his sister's hand. The two of them raced across the clearing and disappeared into the house.

CHAPTER 9

Skeleton Keys

Henry and Jessie took the stone steps to the tower two at a time. Light on their feet, they didn't make a sound until they reached a landing. There they stopped to catch their breath near a small window.

"We're safe for now," Henry whispered. "William is in the gardening shed. Hilda's outside somewhere."

Jessie leaned against the wall. "My heart is about to burst out of me," she said. "We made it. Let's find Benny and Violet. They were pretty brave getting up here so fast."

Henry and Jessie climbed to the next floor.

"Here's the door." Jessie gave it a push.

She and Henry looked around the silent room. The long, narrow windows didn't let in much light. All they could see were the large white shapes of old furniture covered in sheets. Cobwebs hung down from the tall ceiling.

Jessie brushed one aside so it wouldn't get caught in her hair. "Where are Violet and Benny?"

"Down here," a muffled voice answered from under a lump in the corner.

Henry and Jessie walked over. The sheet moved, then two faces peeked out.

"Hey, you two!" Henry helped his brother and Violet slide out from under a huge bed. "We thought you deserted us."

Benny dusted off his hair. "We thought you were William or Hilda or the Walking Skeleton, so we hid under there."

The children tiptoed to the windows,

which overlooked the property and Shady Lake as well.

"This is perfect," Jessie said. "After William and Hilda leave for the day, we'll go back to get our sleeping bags and backpacks, then tidy up a little."

Henry pulled out his binoculars from under his jacket. "I'm glad I brought these. We can see all the way down to the lake and the driveway from the other side. If anything funny is going on, we'll see it. Uh-oh, Hilda's heading to the house with William."

"Shhh," Violet said when she heard something downstairs. She put her head near the old-fashioned heating vent built into the floor. "Listen. They're in the hallway outside the room below here."

The words weren't too clear, but the Aldens recognized William's and Hilda's voices.

"Now that you have all the measurements, how long do you think the job will take?" the Aldens heard William ask. "I need to get everything done fast."

Hilda didn't answer right away. Her voice

was softer, so the Aldens had a harder time hearing her words. ". . . removing it, getting it to the foundry. Making a copy takes a long time. I wish I never told you about . . . "

The Aldens heard a hand bang against a table. "We don't have a long time," he said, so loudly he almost seemed to be in the same room.

Hilda sounded upset and spoke quietly. The Aldens could catch only a few words. ". . . understand . . . need to . . . back . . . why can't . . . Charlotte . . . now."

"Look, I know what I'm doing," William said plainly. "You don't need to know all the details. Can you do what I asked or not?"

The front door slammed. When the children ran to the window, they saw Hilda run from the house and down the driveway. William left shortly afterward.

"What did she say?" Benny asked Violet.

"I couldn't tell," Violet answered softly. "She mentioned a foundry, so it must have something to do with the statues or something like that. Artists sometimes bring statues to a foundry to have molds made of their statues. After that, it's pretty easy to make copies from the molds."

Jessie opened the window. In the distance she heard one car start, then another. "I think they took the Clover Dodge statue to copy it. But it doesn't belong to them. It belongs to Charlotte. We have to tell her soon."

Henry went from window to window aiming his binoculars down the driveway. "It's probably safe to go out and bring our things up now. That'll give us plenty of time to see what's going on in this house while Hilda and William are gone."

After the children aired the room out, they returned to the beach for their packs and sleeping bags.

That's when Jessie heard a motorboat coming close. "Hide!" she told the other children. "Greeny's boat is headed to the dock. He must be coming from the store. I sure hope Max doesn't sniff us out back here. I have the extra food we brought."

"I've got a good idea," Benny said. "I'll

throw one of our extra sandwiches way over there. If Max finds it, he won't come looking for us."

"Good thinking, buddy." Henry and the other children scrunched themselves behind a thick clump of pine trees and bushes.

Soon they heard Greeny's boat slow down, then stop. The children pushed away a branch ever so slightly. What was Greeny going to do next?

"Okay, Max," Greeny said to his dog. "We're safe for a while. Now's our chance to really clear out a few things — a few crates' worth, at least."

The Aldens barely breathed. They heard Max yipping with excitement when he discovered the sandwich Benny had tossed away from the hideout.

"Maxilla!" Greeny yelled. "Don't eat that! Ugh. Too late. You are nothing but a canine garbage disposal. I just hope you don't get sick. I'm putting you on the leash."

Even on a leash, Max smelled food and came awfully close to where the Aldens were hiding.

"Get up here, Max. I'm not letting you run off again." Greeny led Max toward the steps. "I may not have a whole lot of time."

The Aldens waited behind the pine trees for a very long minute.

"Let's follow Greeny now instead of bringing back our things," Jessie suggested. "He's getting something to put in all those crates I see in the boat. I don't know if it's parts of statues or skeletons or what, but now's our chance to follow him."

The children wondered if Greeny would turn off on the secret path. But he didn't stop at all until he reached the gardening shed. "Sorry, Max, but I can't have you barking and running around. You have to stay in here for now. I'll be back for you later."

"Poor thing," Violet whispered when Max began to whine after Greeny shut the door. "He sounds just like Watch when we won't let him play outside with us."

With Max out of the way, the Aldens felt safer in following Greeny into the house. He unlocked the door to Dr. Tibbs's study.

Shutting the door, he locked it from inside the room.

"I know what we can do," Henry whispered. "Let's go upstairs. If we're lucky, there may be a heating vent up there. Maybe we can see into the room."

By now the Aldens knew where many of the creaky floorboards were and avoided them. They found the room above the study. A thick carpet covered most of it.

"Good, Greeny won't be able to hear us walking around," Jessie whispered. She found a corner where the carpet had been cut to let in the heat through a vent. She signaled the others to come over as quietly as possible and huddle around the vent.

When they looked through the grille of the vent, the children saw the top of Greeny's head directly below. They could see him placing skulls, skeletons, and other kinds of bones into his crates.

The Aldens didn't need to discuss what to do next. In an instant, they ran from the room and down the stairs so fast, Greeny never had a chance to get away.

When Greeny opened the door, the Aldens stood there blocking him.

Greeny couldn't move. In his arms was a milk crate piled with skeleton bones. "I'm not even going to lie about what I'm doing," he told the Aldens.

"Good," Jessie said. "Then maybe you'd better explain what you're doing and why. We already saw one skull in your boat. Where are you going with the rest of them?"

Greeny stared at the children for a long time. "Okay, I might as well tell you the truth. You and your relatives can decide what to do about it. I noticed that after Charlotte hired Mason and that woman — "

Henry had something to say. "Wait a minute. Charlotte didn't hire Mr. Mason; he volunteered."

"Hmmm," Greeny said. "Well, maybe Charlotte should have wondered why an architect would volunteer to do something for free — not that I have any idea. All I care about is Dr. Tibbs's collection. Some of it

has disappeared, and I'd bet anything that those two are to blame."

Henry stepped closer to Greeny. "How do you know that? Right now you're the thief, not Mr. Mason and Hilda. Even Mister Bones was taken. He wasn't yours to take, or anybody's."

Now it was Greeny's turn to look upset. "I know, that's why I'm here. After Mister Bones disappeared along with a wild horse skull from out West, I just knew I had to move the whole collection to a safe place — my cabin. I came in here this morning and installed a lock on the door so nothing else would disappear. There are rare skeletons that Dr. Tibbs collected on his travels around the world. Now I'm taking them for safekeeping. You can tell Charlotte that, too."

"No," Violet said. "If you took these things, you'll need to tell Charlotte yourself — tomorrow when she gets back. We're going to find Mister Bones."

Greeny's mouth opened. "Where?"

"We'll let you know tomorrow," Jessie

answered. "Now please put those crates back and give us the keys. Both of them. We're spending the night here."

Though Greeny Owen was many years older than the Aldens, he obeyed them without any more protest. He carried the crate of skeletons back to the study, pulled the door shut, and locked it. Then he dropped both keys in Jessie's waiting hand and went off to get Max.

The children didn't have Mister Bones just yet, but they had discovered that Greeny Owen was one of their thieves. Now they just had to catch the others.

CHAPTER 10

Alive in Dead Man's Cave

After the sun went down, the Aldens turned on their flashlights. The beams cast shadows everywhere.

"At least we don't have to tiptoe around," Henry said as he and his brother and sisters explored the old house.

The children stayed close together so they wouldn't waste their flashlight batteries. When they came to Dr. Tibbs's study, they hesitated at the door.

"We can go in now that I have the keys," Jessie said to Violet and Benny. "But we don't have to unless you want to."

Henry spotted two camp lanterns on a table in the hall. "Mr. Mason must have left those. Let's turn them on to brighten up this place." Henry pushed the lantern switches. "There, now it looks almost like a people house, not a skeleton house."

Jessie found the keys to Dr. Tibbs's study in her pocket. She unlocked the room.

"Oooh, now I'm not so sure about coming in here," Benny said, taking Jessie's hand. "You go first, Henry."

The children stepped into the room and gazed at the shelves and tables of skeletons. The dim light made the bony shapes seem scarier than ever.

"By the looks of things, about half of the skeletons aren't here anymore," Jessie said. "We know Greeny removed an awful lot of them in those crates."

Violet gazed at the empty window. "I know, but I do think he was telling the truth and that someone else took Mister Bones and some other skeletons. Otherwise, why would he be so upset about them and ex-

cited when we told him we were going to get them back?"

Jessie locked the study again. "Let's look around the rest of the house some more. We'll come back here during the daytime." She took one lantern and led the other children down the hall. When she came to the kitchen, she set the lantern down.

Henry walked over to a wobbly kitchen table where papers and notebooks were scattered on top. "Looks as if Hilda and William set up their work in here." He used his flashlight to get a closer look at the blueprints, notebooks, and papers.

Benny felt braver now that they were in the kitchen and not in the skeleton room. He came over to see what was on the table. That's when he saw something familiar sticking out from one of the sketch pads on the pile. "Look, the pictures I took! How did they get in here?"

Violet had a suggestion. "I don't know, but put them in a safe place right now. When we see Hilda again, tell her you found them."

Benny was glad to have his photos back. "Hey, look at this," he said, turning the pictures over. "Somebody wrote prices on the back. See? The angel statue picture says three thousand dollars. And the picture with the girl statue next to Violet is seven thousand dollars. Is that a lot?"

Henry frowned. "It sure is." He took the picture from Benny and put it down next to Hilda's sketch pad. "The handwriting looks the same."

"Why do you suppose Hilda took Benny's pictures?" Violet asked.

Jessie had a thought. "I have a feeling she or William took them so Charlotte wouldn't have evidence that the statues disappeared while they were in charge."

"Then I'm glad Charlotte and Grandfather are coming here tomorrow morning," Jessie said. "There's a lot to tell them about. Now let's go upstairs and have our extra sandwiches for dinner. We have a big day ahead, and I want to get to sleep early."

*　*　*

The next morning, sunlight poured into the tower room, waking the Aldens one by one. They yawned and stretched and sat up in bed.

"I feel like a princess in a tower," Violet said. "This bed is so tall and so fancy. I slept just as if I were home in Greenfield."

"Well, I sure didn't," Henry said. "I heard noises while it was still dark this morning, but I figured it was just the wind."

Jessie went over to the window after she heard a car. "Hey, guess who's coming up the driveway. Grandfather and Charlotte." She opened the window and waved. "We're up here."

The children scrambled into their clothes and ran down the driveway.

Charlotte gave everyone a big smile. "Well, you children were very brave to sleep in a house filled with skeletons and no electricity."

Benny shook his head. "It's just half filled with skeletons. Some of them got stolen."

Grandfather looked surprised. "What do you mean? We spoke with William last evening. He didn't mention anything missing. Let's go find him. He's in the house already with Hilda, I imagine. Their cars are parked below."

The children went off to look around.

"No one's here except the rest of Dr. Tibbs's skeletons," Jessie said. "But I think I know where they might be. Follow us."

With the children leading the way, Grandfather and Charlotte followed the shortcut path to the gardens.

Charlotte stared at the empty space where the statue of the girl had been. Her face seemed about to crumble.

Jessie took her hand. "Don't worry. We know where the statue is," Jessie said as she linked her arm in Charlotte's. "We need to cross over the main path, then go into the woods on the other side."

Shortly before the Aldens came to Dead Man's Cave, they heard William and Hilda arguing.

"I don't want any part of this," Hilda said. "You told me you only had copies made so the old statues could be put away safely. You can't sell them or even copies of them. They're not yours."

The Aldens crept along until they reached Dead Man's Cave. The rusted door was open, revealing William, Hilda, and Mister Bones, along with several skeletons and statues the children hadn't seen before.

"Sell what?" Charlotte asked when she stepped forward.

Hilda rushed outside, with William right behind her. He tried to shut the door, but Henry was too quick for him.

"Leave it open," Henry said.

"I'm glad you're here," Hilda said to Charlotte. "I just want you to know that I'm not part of William's scheme."

Charlotte frowned anxiously. "What scheme?"

Hilda spoke clearly. "He was going to make copies of your statues and sell the originals. They were made by a famous sculptor named Clover Dodge, and they're worth a lot of money." Hilda looked embarrassed. "I didn't know what was really going on. I only figured it out this morning

— I followed him here to tell him I was quitting." Hilda pointed toward the cave. "The missing statues are all in there."

Charlotte and the Aldens went in to look around. Sure enough, the Clover Dodge statue sat in a corner, looking sad and out of place. Several statues the Aldens hadn't seen also filled the dark space. Only Mister Bones and the wild horse skull seemed at home in Dead Man's Cave.

"Is all this true?" Charlotte asked William, frowning. "How could you do such a thing?"

William Mason scowled and looked down at the ground. "Yeah, it's all true. I wanted to buy the house myself. It's a gold mine, with all those statues. And some of the rare bones are just as valuable. But you beat me to it — and you didn't even know what you had!"

"If you wanted the house yourself, why did you volunteer to help Charlotte?" asked Henry.

"It's like Hilda said. I figured I could sell the statues and rare bones and make myself some money anyway. I figured you'd never notice if some stuff began to disappear."

"But *we* noticed," said Henry.

William Mason glared at the Aldens. "That's right, you kids started snooping around. I untied your boat to try to keep you away from the house. I even hid some skeletons and bones in the woods, hoping that they'd scare you off — but unfortunately it didn't work."

Jessie looked surprised. "We thought Greeny was the one hiding all the skeletons and bones for us to find."

"I'd never do anything like that," came a voice from behind them. Everyone looked up as Greeny and Max suddenly emerged from behind the trees. Greeny wore black pants and his T-shirt with the skull on the front and the bones on the back. "I followed you here," Greeny said. "I had a hunch these kids knew something about where all the missing bones were. I suspected Mason was behind the whole thing! I'll admit I tried to scare you and your family away from Skeleton Point. I snuck up on these kids the first time I saw them at Skeleton Point and tried to spook them."

"But you can't scare us off that easy," said Benny.

"I figured that out pretty quick," Greeny said. He looked down at the ground. "I'm the one who hid those Halloween skulls in your bike helmets," he said to the Aldens. "And I planted a skeleton by your car, too, Charlotte. I just wanted to save Dr. Tibbs's collection by keeping people away. But I would *never* have used any of the real bones to do something like that — they're too valuable!"

Charlotte moved toward Greeny. They were quite a contrast with each other. Charlotte with her white curly hair, her tweed jacket, and pearl earrings didn't seem to have a thing in common with Greeny Owen in his skull shirt, ponytail, and skull earring. "I'm glad that you told me, Greeny. I hope that now we can be friends — and I hope you know I care about Dr. Tibbs's collection as much as you do."

"Hey, what about Mr. Mason?" Benny asked.

William Mason was slowly backing up, trying to escape from the group without anyone noticing.

When Charlotte turned to look at William Mason, the smile disappeared from her face. "I don't believe we'll be needing your services anymore, Mr. Mason. And you can be sure that I'll be contacting the authorities to inform them of what you tried to do here. I don't think you'll be getting any more architecture jobs anytime soon. Now please leave the property — and be thankful I'm not calling the police."

William Mason opened his mouth to respond, but he couldn't think of anything to say. He spun around and hurried away into the woods.

"Well, children, I guess we'll need to get all these statues and skeletons back to the house," Charlotte said, in a happier voice. "Thank you so much for finding them for me! I had no idea that they were made by a well-known sculptor." She turned to Grandfather. "James, does the name Clover Dodge ring a bell with you?" she asked.

Grandfather looked at his cousin Charlottee as if remembering something long ago. "Dodge? Yes, yes," Grandfather began. "I vaguely recall the name — that was the name of the original family that owned Skeleton Point — before it was Skeleton Point, that is. But I had no idea she was a sculptor as well."

A smile slowly lit up Charlotte's face.

"What's funny?" Benny asked.

Charlotte sighed. "In some ways, I'm better off than I was before all this happened! I have all these valuable statues back, including the ones I didn't even know were missing. And now I have experts — Greeny and Hilda — who can help me bring Skeleton Point back to life."

Benny walked over to Mister Bones. He was hanging just inside the doorway of Dead Man's Cave. "Did you hear that, Mister Bones? You might be coming back to life."

GERTRUDE CHANDLER WARNER discovered when she was teaching that many readers who like an exciting story could find no books that were both easy and fun to read. She decided to try to meet this need, and her first book, *The Boxcar Children*, quickly proved she had succeeded.

Miss Warner drew on her own experiences to write the mystery. As a child she spent hours watching trains go by on the tracks opposite her family home. She often dreamed about what it would be like to set up housekeeping in a caboose or freight car — the situation the Alden children find themselves in.

When Miss Warner received requests for more adventures involving Henry, Jessie, Violet, and Benny Alden, she began additional stories. In each, she chose a special setting and introduced unusual or eccentric characters who liked the unpredictable.

While the mystery element is central to each of Miss Warner's books, she never thought of them as strictly juvenile mysteries. She liked to stress the Aldens' independence and resourcefulness and their solid New England devotion to using up and making do. The Aldens go about most of their adventures with as little adult supervision as possible — something else that delights young readers.

Miss Warner lived in Putnam, Connecticut, until her death in 1979. During her lifetime, she received hundreds of letters from girls and boys telling her how much they liked her books.